W9-AAX-691

For Adrian, without whom I never would have finished this book, and for Tao, without whom I would have finished a lot faster

Look here, Tao, you naughty cat,
You really are a dirty rat!

You know it's very, very rude
to eat my Art as if 'twere food,

so now two locks upon my door
will keep you out forevermore.

Please don't howl — it's very grating —
look, my editor is waiting!

Oh, one last feather, now go and play —
I've got to finish this today.

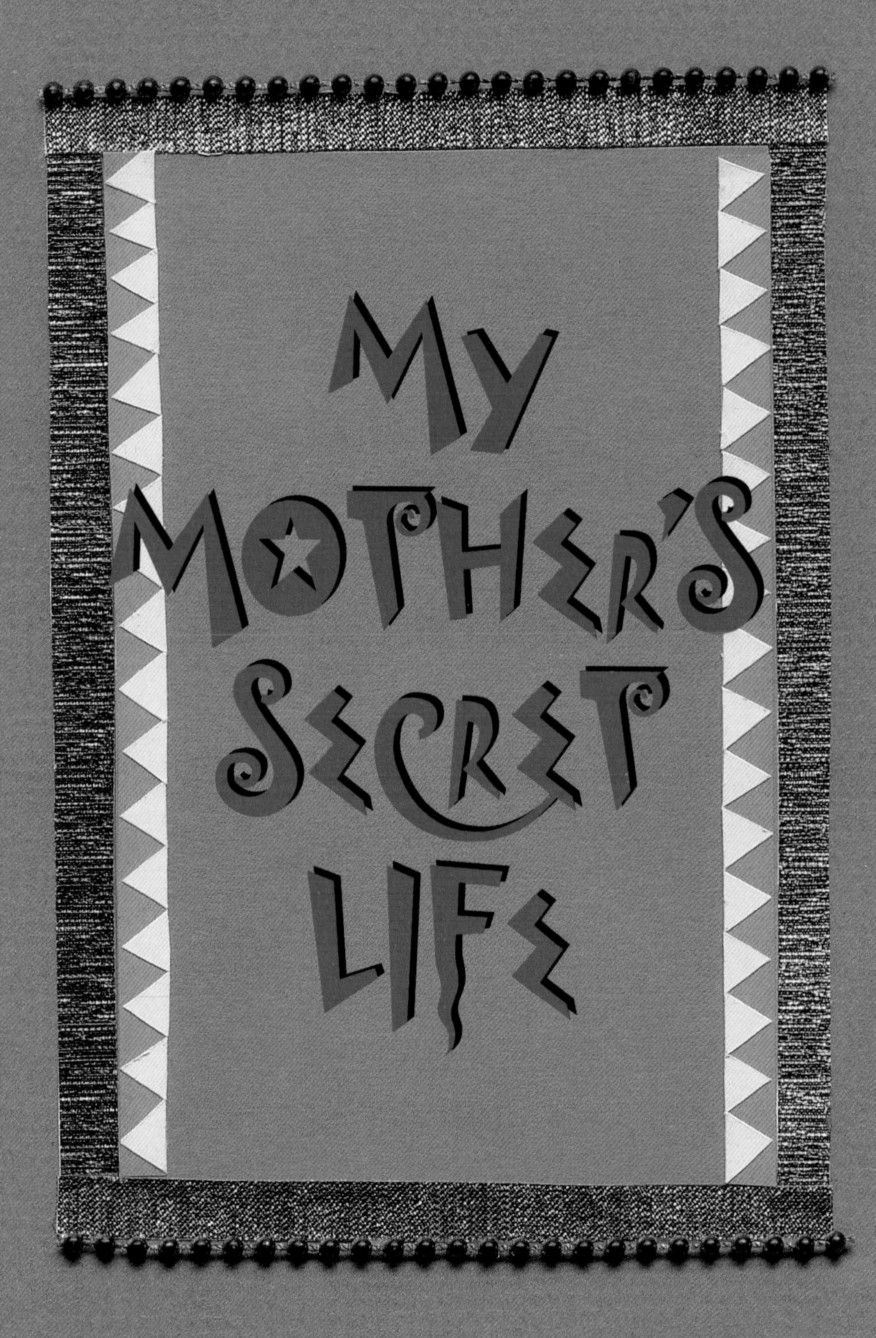
MY
MOTHER'S
SECRET
LIFE

First Edition

Library of Congress Cataloging-in-Publication Data

Emberley, Rebecca.
My mother's secret life / Rebecca Emberley. — 1st ed.
p. cm.
Summary: A young daughter, never dreaming that Mother does anything more than clean the house and take care of her, begins to see things differently.
ISBN 0-316-23496-6
[1. Mothers and daughters — Fiction. 2. Secrets — Fiction. 3. Dreams — Fiction. 4. Circus — Fiction.] I. Title.
PZ7.E5665My 1998
[E] — DC21 97-19931

10 9 8 7 6 5 4 3 2 1

SC

Published simultaneously in Canada
by Little, Brown & Company (Canada) Limited

Printed in Hong Kong

My Mother's Secret Life

Rebecca Emberley

Little, Brown and Company
Boston New York Toronto London

The dog threw up on the carpet.

The cat ate the frosting off the cake.

I broke my mother's pearl necklace while I was supposed to be cleaning my room.

"That's it!" my mother cried. Holding her head, my mother said, "Enough. This place looks like a three-ring circus!"

The dog looked sad. The cat meowed, and her breath smelled a lot like vanilla. "I am going to my room!" said my mother, grabbing her hat on the way up the stairs.

"So long," I said.

I got out my paints and painted the refrigerator. Next, I made myself a snack.

There was a lot of thumping and bumping from upstairs, but my mother did not come downstairs to clean the kitchen. So I decided to take a nap.

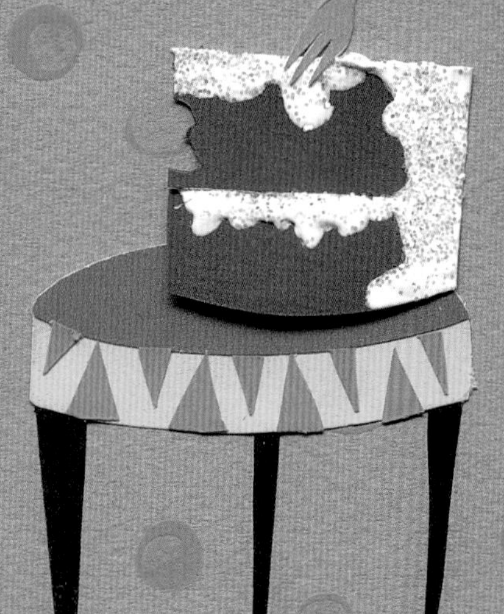

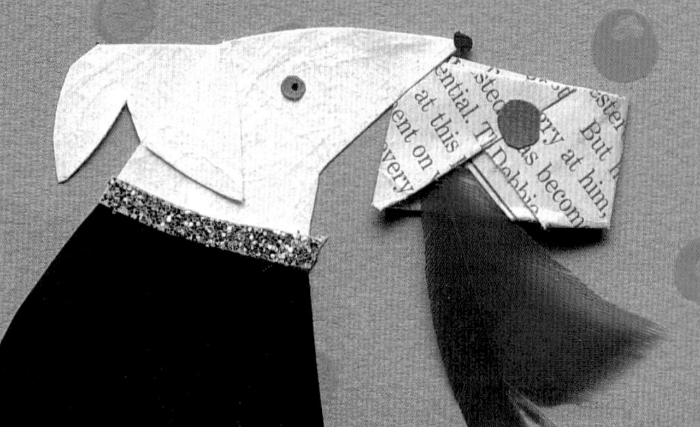

Garcia Abrego, allegedly a top

I dreamt I was at the circus. I was eating popcorn and holding a stuffed animal on a stick. Acrobats were doing tricks.

I heard music, and three spotted horses pranced into a big ring. There were ladies in fancy costumes. As they raced past, their feathers tickled my nose, and I smelled

Next came the clowns. I laughed and laughed. I liked the clown in the black hat the best.

The lights went out. I looked up. High at the top of the tent there was a spotlight. I saw a swing.

There was a lady hanging upside down.
Her costume sparkled and shined.

I stood up to get a better look, and my popcorn spilled on the man in front of me. He was not happy. He turned and began to roar at me, and I was afraid. He looked as though he might bite me! People were yelling.

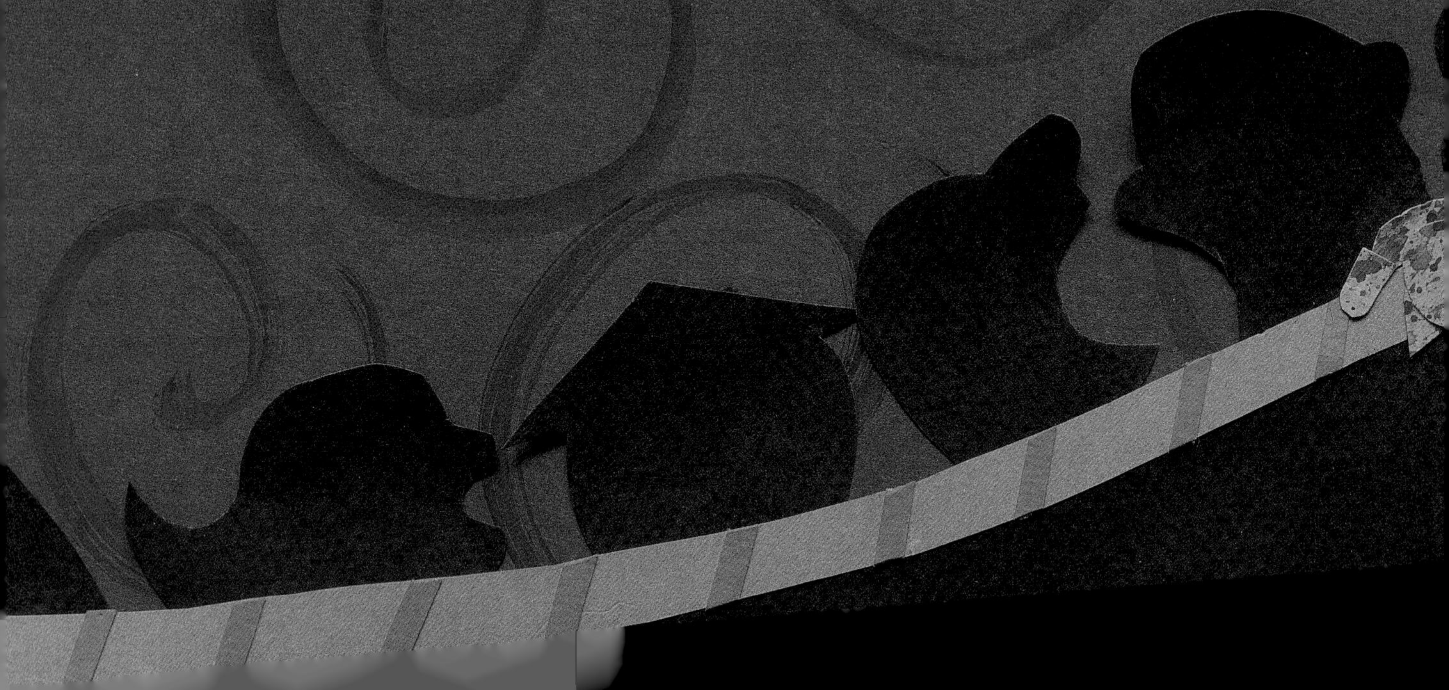

Suddenly, I heard a noise and the air swirled around me.

"MOTHER!" I cried.

"Who else?" said the lady hanging by her heels, as she swept me up and away.

I opened my eyes. I saw my mother's smile. "Mother," I said. "I dreamt we were at the circus."

"How exciting!" said Mother. "I love the circus." The dog smiled. The cat yawned, and her breath smelled a little like popcorn.